Acting Edition

I0591739

The Last Resort

by Tom Ziegler

THE LAST RESORT was first produced by the Triangle Theater Company at the Church of the Holy Trinity on January 19, 1988. The performance was directed by Will Cantler with sets by set designer Bob Phillips, costumes by costume designer Amanda J. Klein, lights by lighting designer Danianne Mizzy. The Production Stage Manager was Anne M. Cantler. The cast was as follows:

MARJORIE KENDRICK ....Meg Mundy

HENRY DOWNS ....Fred Burrell

ISABEL LOWERY...................................Kathryn Eames

DOTTIE BARTEL .... Marjorie Lovett

ABE FISHMAN...................................Albert S. Bennett

ROSE FERGUSON.................................Gerri Beckham

STEVEN KENDRICK............................... Rob Donohoe

MARY DILLARD....................................... Anne Stone

CHARACTERS

MARJORIE KENDRICK – Senior Citizen

HENRY DOWNS – Senior Citizen

ISABEL LOWERY – Senior Citizen

DOTTIE BARTEL – Senior Citizen

ABE WAXMAN – Senior Citizen

ROSE FERGUSON – Senior Citizen

STEVEN KENDRICK – Thirties, Marjorie's son

MARY MUELLER – Late thirties, a nurse

SETTING

The entire action takes place in the single setting of the recreation room and outdoor patio of Sunset Terrace, a posh convalescent home for the elderly, located somewhere on Long Island, New York. The time is early autumn, 1988.

There are contemporary furniture and accessories: tables, chairs, large television/stereo console. The entrance to the room is through swinging double doors up right. Up left is a closet with games and craft items. A door on the right wall leads to a bathroom. Down left double doors lead to an outdoor patio equipped with groupings of exterior furniture. The recreation room is decorated in the bright warm colors of modern institutional.

TIME

Act I, Scene One
An early autumn afternoon not long ago.
Act I, Scene Two
Lunch time three weeks later.
Act II, Scene One
Evening, a week later.
Act II, Scene Two
The next morning.

ACT I

Scene One

(Music from one of the "big bands," like Duke Ellington, Glenn Miller, Paul Whiteman.*)

(The recreation room and outside patio of the Sunset Terrace assisted living and nursing facility. It's an early afternoon in the fall of 1988.)

*(***ISABEL LOWERY*** is sitting on the patio next to* ***HENRY DOWNS***. *Although delicate and refined, there's something about* ***ISABEL*** *that seems askew. Perhaps it's her dress that's not buttoned quite right, her hair that hasn't seen a comb in several days.* ***HENRY*** *wears a faded print shirt, a pair of worn, faded slacks, a hearing aid on his coke-bottle-thick glasses. Holding a pad of paper and a pen, he's poised to write.)*

(Inside the recreation room, ***ROSE FERGUSON***, ***DOTTIE BARTEL***, *and* ***ABE WAXMAN*** *are sleeping in various chairs around the room.*

---

* A license to produce *The Last Resort* does not include a performance license for any third-party or copyrighted music. Licensees should create an original composition or use music in the public domain. For further information, please see the Music and Third-Party Materials Use Note on page iii.

*ROSE is dressed in a flannel robe and has a brightly-colored quilt over her lap. Her wrists are bound to the arms of a wheel chair. **DOTTIE BARTEL**, wearing a navy suit, hat, white gloves, and matching accessories, looks as if she were about to head off to a matinee. A small suitcase sits on the floor next to her chair. **ABE WAXMAN** would look dapper in his tailored slacks, bow tie, V-neck sweater, if he weren't slumped on the sofa with mouth agape.)*

ISABEL. This certainly is wonderful of you to help me, Henry.

HENRY. No problem. Okay, I got "Monday, October 2nd, 1988. Dear Mr. Gilmore."

ISABEL. It's criminal how far behind I've gotten in my correspondence. I can imagine what people are thinking of me.

HENRY. Let's go on. "Dear Mr. Gilmore."

ISABEL. *(Holding out her hands.)* If I could just keep my hands from trembling so. Isn't it time Mary was by with the medications?

HENRY. Isabel, you're wandering. "Dear Mr. Gilmore."

ISABEL. Who?

HENRY. The letter you were dictating. I got "Monday, October 2nd, 1988. Dear Mr. Gilmore." What's next?

ISABEL. Oh, yes. I'm sorry.

HENRY. No problem.

ISABEL. Dear Mr. Gilmore.

HENRY. I got that.

ISABEL. God bless you for the beautiful radio I won at your "Golden Years Bizarre."

*(**HENRY** writes.)*

I am seventy-nine years old and a resident of Sunset Terrace home for seniors. I spent forty years of my life teaching little first grade boys and girls to read and write and count. All of my people are gone now, so it's nice to know there are those who care about the elderly. God bless you for your kindness to an old forgotten lady.

HENRY. *(Writing.)* ...old forgotten lady.

ISABEL. My roommate, Ethyl, is ninety-one years old and has always had a radio of her own, but she'd never let me listen to it. The other day her radio fell and broke into tiny little pieces. It was awful.

The poor thing, her eyes were filled with tears. She looked at me and asked, can I please listen to your new radio?" I smiled and said, "Ethyl," I said, "fuck you."

*(**HENRY** stops writing.)*

Very truly yours, Isabel Lowery.

*(There's a moment. Then **HENRY** tears the paper from the pad and crumples it into a ball. **ISABEL** laughs.)*

HENRY. Suppose you think you're funny.

ISABEL. That's such an old joke I can't believe you haven't heard it.

*(**HENRY** stands.)*

I'm sorry. Don't be angry with me. I'm just so bored.

*(**HENRY** goes into the recreation room; **ISABEL** follows.)*

I know, why don't we play poker.

HENRY. I don't want to play poker. You cheat.

ISABEL. I don't cheat. You've just had a string of bad luck.

HENRY. String of bad luck? I haven't won a game in three years!

ISABEL. *(Sitting at the card table.)* Come on. A couple hands. 'Til the Soaps come on.

> *(**HENRY** hesitates. Then sits and shuffles the cards. **ISABEL** takes a pack of cigarettes from her pocket.)*

HENRY. Call the game.

ISABEL. Why am I so tired all the time? And these headaches. Help me get a cigarette out of this stupid pack.

HENRY. You're not supposed to smoke in here.

ISABEL. So what?

HENRY. *(Standing.)* If you insist on breaking the rules, you'll have to do it without me.

ISABEL. Don't leave.

HENRY. Then call the game.

ISABEL. Five card stud, Jacks or better to open. Twenty buck ante.

> *(They each throw a chip in the center of the table.)*

I wish Mary'd come. I know it's time for our pills.

HENRY. *(Dealing.)* Mary's admitting a new resident.

ISABEL. *(Yawning.)* Who?

HENRY. Some wealthy woman from Westhampton.

ISABEL. How do you know?

HENRY. How many cards you want?

ISABEL. *(Yawning.)* I don't care. Two.

> *(**ISABEL** closes her eyes.)*

HENRY. Two for Isabel and the dealer takes...three. The woman had a stroke. Pretty bad. Can't walk. You going to open or what? Izzy?

> (**ISABEL** *sits there asleep holding her hand of cards.*)

Guess it's up to you, Henry. Okay, I'll just open here with –

> (*He throws a chip into the pot.*)

– fifty dollars. You going to see my fifty dollars, Isabel? Sure you are.

> (*He takes a chip from Isabel's pile and adds it to the pot.*)

And you're going to raise me another fifty. And me,

> (*Tossing chips into the pot.*)

I'll see your fifty and raise you – Hmm, let's think about this for a minute.

> (*He looks at the other people in the room to make sure they're asleep. He gets up and quietly moves behind* **ISABEL**. *He leans over and just as he is about to get a peek at her cards, he hears something.*)

STEVEN. (*Offstage.*) And down here's the recreation room. You're going to love it, Mom, just love it.

> (**HENRY** *turns quickly and tiptoes out to the terrace, closing the doors after himself. He stands near the door so he can eavesdrop.*)

> (*Nurse* **MARY MUELLER** *backs into the room pulling a wheelchair occupied by the newest arrival to Sunset Terrace,* **MARJORIE KENDRICK. MARY** *is in her late thirties, very*

sweet and ever so cheerful. **MARJORIE** *is an attractive woman, late sixties. A recent stroke has partially paralyzed the left side of her body. She is accompanied by her son,* **STEVEN***, thirties, dressed in casual but tailored clothes.)*

STEVEN. Oh, yes. Look at this room.

MARJORIE. Steven.

MARY. Most of our residents, the ambulatory ones, spend a lot of time in here. You'll notice –

MARJORIE. Steven! I mean it, get me out of here!

MARY. Now, now, Mrs. Kendrick. Mind if I call you Marjorie?

STEVEN. Just take a minute to look around, Mom.

MARY. Your son's right, Marjorie.

STEVEN. When we drove up. Did you notice the grounds? And the building, the layout, there's only one word for this place.

(Trying to think of the word.)

MARY. *(Helping.)* Homey?

STEVEN. No, I was thinking of...homey, yes. This room, for example. So bright and...Look, cable TV, VCR, a game closet. And check out this stereo. Compact disks. Lawerence Welk, Mitch Miller, Liberace.

MARJORIE. Listen to me, goddamnit! You get me the hell out of here or I'll –

MARY. You might mention our fine collection of "gospel music."

STEVEN. And the food. They let me sneak a taste last week. Believe me, my Patsy could take lessons from their chef. What else?

MARY. The spa?

STEVEN. That's right, the spa! Sauna, jacuzzi. Resort! That's the word I was looking for.

MARJORIE. You like it here, Steven? You like it that much?

STEVEN. I do. Very, very much.

MARJORIE. Good. Then you move here!

STEVEN. Mother, listen to me. Just take a minute –

MARJORIE. Did I see a pay phone in the hall?

MARY. There're two of them on every floor.

MARJORIE. Terrific. Give me a quarter, Steven, I'm calling a cab.

STEVEN. For the love of god, you just had a stroke.

(To **MARY.***)*

She was unconscious for weeks. Doctor said it was a miracle she pulled through.

MARJORIE. Miracle, my foot. I pulled myself through it. And just when I was ready to leave that hospital you kidnap me and bring me here.

STEVEN. You're half-paralyzed.

MARJORIE. I have a little trouble with my left side. Big deal. Everything else my eyes, my ears, my nose, my – Good lord, what's that smell?

MARY. Smell?

(She tests the air.)

Oh. Yes.

(Smiles. Pulls out a can of air freshener and begins spraying the room.)

You two make yourself at home, I'll only be a minute.

*(**MARY** hurries over to **ABE**.)*

STEVEN. *(Trying his best to distract **MARJORIE**.)* Soon as we finish here I'll take you down to the kitchen. The aromas coming out of that room will –

MARY. *(Shaking **ABE**.)* Wake up, Abe. Time to go back to your room.

ABE. What are you doing shaking me? Take your hands off me!

MARY. Abe, you had an accident.

ABE. Accident? What am I doing, driving down the turnpike?

MARY. I'm talking about –

(She whispers.)

ABE. Oh. That's no accident. The food, that's what it is.

*(As they pass **MARJORIE**, **ABE** reaches out and grabs **MARJORIE**'s arm.)*

Listen to me. If you can get word to the outside tell them that they're poisoning us with the food. Especially the meatloaf. I'll tell you, if Job had been forced to eat their meatloaf, he'd have renounced God!

MARY. Abe, you don't settle down I'm going to give you a shot.

ABE. So shoot me. Please.

MARY. *(Turning back to **STEVEN**.)* You'll have to excuse, Mr. Waxman. He likes to show off in front of new people. Why don't you come with me, Mr. Kendrick? Your mother's room is almost ready, in the meantime, you can finish signing the admission forms.

MARJORIE. Steven, for the last time, I want to go home!

ABE. Steven, be a good son, take your mother home.

MARY. *(Taking hold of* **MARJORIE***'s wrist.)* Oh, yes. Before I leave you alone just let me –

(She takes a plastic identification bracelet out of her pocket and fastens it to **MARJORIE***'s wrist.)*

MARJORIE. What are you doing?

MARY. It's an identification bracelet, Marjorie. It has your name and your physician's name and –

ABE. *(Poking his head through the door.)* And it says "If not claimed in thirty days..."

MARY. *(Sweetly.)* Abe, please behave yourself.

(Turning back, smiling.)

Why don't you get acquainted with your new neighbors Marjorie. Attention everyone!

(Clapping her hands.)

This is Marjorie Kendrick, our newest resident. I'm sure you'll all make her feel right at home.

*(***MARY*** exits. None of the residents stir.)*

MARJORIE. Please, Steven. Don't leave me here.

STEVEN. I'm only going to the office.

MARJORIE. What do I have to do, beg?

STEVEN. I'll be back in a few minutes. In the meantime. Like the nurse said. Make friends.

(He hurries out.)

MARJORIE. Steven!

*(***MARJORIE*** slumps in her chair, sitting for a while with her back to the audience. Slowly she turns the wheelchair around and surveys the other people in the room.)*

MARJORIE. Excuse me. Can anyone lend me a quarter?

>*(There is no response. She tries again.)*

Hello? Is anybody there?

>*(Still no response.)*

My new neighbors. They must hire someone to come in once a week to dust them.

>*(**MARJORIE** tries to negotiate the wheelchair toward the hall door by moving one wheel at a time with her right hand. She gets nowhere.)*

Damn thing.

>*(**HENRY** hesitates a moment, then opens the terrace door and enters.)*

HENRY. *(Clears his throat.)* Afternoon.

>*(**MARJORIE** turns toward **HENRY**, nods.)*

Downs.

MARJORIE. Pardon me?

HENRY. Henry Downs.

MARJORIE. Oh.

HENRY. You?

MARJORIE. Marjorie. Kendrick.

HENRY. *(Pointing to his hearing aid.)* Have to speak up.

MARJORIE. *(A little louder.)* Of course. Marjorie Kendrick!

HENRY. Marjorie Kent?

MARJORIE. *(Holding out her right wrist.)* Here, read it for yourself.

HENRY. *(Looking closely.)* Kendrick. Oh, you must be the new resident.

MARJORIE. I'm not staying.

HENRY. None of us are, Marge. None of us are.

MARJORIE. I mean I don't belong in a place like this. There's nothing really wrong with me.

HENRY. Grim Reaper's waiting room. That's what we call this place.

MARJORIE. Maybe you could help me. I'd like to call a taxi. If you could just push me –

HENRY. Listen, Marge, I make it a point to keep my nose out of other people's affairs.

MARJORIE. But my son's trying to dump me here, damnit!

HENRY. Try not to make too much noise. Don't want to wake Isabel.

MARJORIE. Who?

HENRY. One with the cards. She's an old maid schoolteacher and you know how crotchety they can be.

> *(A beat.)*

You're not an old maid schoolteacher, are you?

MARJORIE. No.

HENRY. Didn't think so. Look here.

> *(Showing **MARJORIE** his cards.)*

Ace high flush. What would you say're the odds of me beating her?

MARJORIE. I'm sorry I don't know anything about poker. I've played a little bridge but –

HENRY. She beats me every time. Owe her more'n a hundred thousand dollars. She takes advantage of me cause I can't see too good. Hey, maybe when Izzy wakes up we can all –

MARJORIE. I told you, I'm not staying. Like it or not, when Steven gets back he's going to take me home!

HENRY. Steven? That your son's name?

MARJORIE. That's one of the things I call him.

HENRY. Don't have any children myself. Lived alone. Then my hearing started to go, my eyes. I was in a hospital for a while. Nothing much. Hernia. And then they sent me here. Government pays the bills.

MARJORIE. How long have you been here?

HENRY. Four years, three months and twenty-two days.

MARJORIE. Four years!

HENRY. Three months and twenty-two days.

MARJORIE. How have you been able to stand it?

HENRY. Oh, I'm used to places like this.

MARJORIE. Used to it? How can you get used to a...prison?

HENRY. *(Suddenly becoming defensive.)* What?

MARJORIE. I said –

HENRY. Someone told you about me, didn't they?

MARJORIE. No, of course not. I merely –

HENRY. By god, that makes me angry. That was thirty years ago!

MARJORIE. Mr. Downs, I don't have the faintest idea what you're talking about.

 (Trying to wheel herself toward the door.)

Now if you'll excuse me, I –

HENRY. You mean it? Nobody told you I was an ex-con?

MARJORIE. No.

(A beat.)

A what?

(Turning back.)

HENRY. Don't look at me like that. I didn't kill anyone or even... It was...embezzlement. Spent eight years in the federal prison at Otisville.

MARJORIE. I see.

HENRY. It's not that I needed the money. I had a good job. In a bank. Assistant Vice President. Good salary, bright future. Then I...I met this...

MARJORIE. Woman.

HENRY. You can see where this is going. Name was Sylvia. Beautiful. Kind of beauty makes a man... Sylvia liked pretty things. Expensive, pretty things. Go ahead, laugh. Everybody does.

MARJORIE. I'm not laughing.

HENRY. *(Looking close.)* I can see the smile on your face. Least it looks like a smile. Why is it only half there?

> *(**MARJORIE** quickly puts her hand over her mouth.)*

Sorry, I didn't mean – It's very becoming. It is. Half a smile. Reminds me of...*The Mona Lisa*?

MARJORIE. I had a stroke.

HENRY. Ahh. Nasty things. Lost two of my roommates that way.

MARJORIE. It's only my left half, and that's getting better. When this first happened I couldn't even cry out of my left eye. But now, I can wiggle my nose, wink both eyes and raise my index finger.

HENRY. You'd be great at an auction.

MARJORIE. They tell me I'd been overdoing it. You see, I had been cleaning my house.

HENRY. You got a stroke from house cleaning? You must be very neat.

MARJORIE. It was more than just cleaning, I was "emerging." My husband, Carter? We had been married forty years, and – You'd probably rather not hear this.

HENRY. Oh, it's all right. Your husband – Carter – uh, how long since he –

MARJORIE. Almost two years. Most of that time I just sat, staring into space. Then a friend gave me this book, *The Emerging Widow*. You familiar with it? No, I suppose not. Anyway, the book said I needed a fresh start. Told me to clean out the house, sell everything – furniture, linens, clothes. Then redecorate. So, I did. That's when, you know, this.

HENRY. Guess you're looking forward to getting back to it.

MARJORIE. Oh, I am.

*(She stops, looks over at **ROSE**, whispers.)*

Henry. That woman over there. She's gone to the bathroom right there on the floor.

HENRY. *(Not looking.)* That's Rose.

MARJORIE. But shouldn't we wake her?

HENRY. She gets all embarrassed when it happens so we pretty much ignore it.

MARJORIE. Poor woman. Why is she tied to her chair like that?

HENRY. Restraints. They use them sometimes. Wheelchairs, beds. Probably be taking Rose to the second floor one of these days.

MARJORIE. The second floor?

HENRY. Where the patients are. We're residents down here. Upstairs they're patients.

MARJORIE. You mean there's a difference?

HENRY. Big difference. You think it smells down here, go upstairs. Decay. That's what you smell up there. You stay away from the second floor, Marge. Only one way out of there. Down the service elevator and into the hearse.

>   *(A phone rings somewhere offstage.* **DOTTIE** *struggles to her feet.)*

DOTTIE. Time to go, time to go.

HENRY. No, Dottie. That's just the phone at the nurse's station.

DOTTIE. What a pretty, sunny day. I knew Nancy would pick a pretty, sunny day.

>   *(She moves slowly toward the hall door.)*

Good thing I packed this morning. It was that last novena to the Blessed Virgin, that's what did it. Goodbye Henry. Goodbye, Isabel.

ISABEL. What? Time for pills?

DOTTIE. Just me, Isabel. Nancy's here. Where's Abe? I want to say goodbye to him, too.

HENRY. He isn't here, Dottie.

DOTTIE. Really? Smells like he is. Oh, well. Rose, I hate to wake you, but Nancy's here. Goodbye, Rose. I'll write to you.

>   *(She exits.)*

ROSE. *(Waking up, realizing that she's wet.)* Oh, my.

>   *(She leans over and looks at the floor.)*

Oh, my.

(She looks up to see if anyone has noticed.
MARJORIE *is looking at her.)*

ROSE. Oh, my.

(She struggles with the straps on her wrists.)

Oh, my.

(She turns away, slumping down in her chair.)

My, oh my, oh my.

HENRY. Come on, Isabel, it's your bet. I just raised you five
hundred dollars.

ISABEL. *(To* **MARJORIE**.*)* You're new, aren't you? Do you
play cards?

MARJORIE. I'm just visiting.

ISABEL. Sure, sure.

(Getting up.)

What did you say your name was?

MARJORIE. Marjorie.

ISABEL. Here, Marjorie, play my hand while I go get some
aspirin. And don't let Henry peek at your cards. He
pretends to be half-blind so he can cheat.

MARJORIE. But I'm not staying... Alright, perhaps a day
or two.

ISABEL. In that case I'll hurry. Bridge. I'll bet that's your
game. Tell you what, when I get back we'll find a deck
and play a few hands.

(Exiting.)

Penny a point.

MARJORIE. *(Indicating the cards.)* So what do I do
with these?

HENRY. You already know what I have. Just say "I call."

MARJORIE. All right. I call.

HENRY. *(Laying down his cards.)* There you go. Read 'em and weep. Club flush, Ace high.

> *(He starts gathering in the chips.)*

MARJORIE. Wait just one minute. I have

> *(She lays down her cards.)*

four kings.

> *(**HENRY** throws his cards into the air as **MARY** leads **DOTTIE** back into the room. **STEVEN** follows.)*

MARY. Come on, Dottie. Come on back and sit down.

DOTTIE. *(Shuffling back into the room.)* One of the children is probably sick. That must be it.

STEVEN. Your room's ready, Mother. It's a beautiful room. I know you're going to love it.

MARY. Here, Dottie. Doctor wants you to take your pills.

> *(She takes a white cup of pills and puts them in **DOTTIE**'s hand.)*

DOTTIE. She'll be here tomorrow, won't she nurse?

MARY. Here's some water. Be a good girl now, take your pills.

> *(She turns, notices the puddle on the floor.)*

Looks like somebody else had an accident.

ROSE. *(Turning away.)* Oh, my.

MARJORIE. *(To the nurse.)* Is there some place my son and I can be alone?

STEVEN. I told you, your room's ready.

MARY. We don't usually have this many bathroom problems, Mr. Kendrick, but we've lost two of our best aides in the last month.

MARJORIE. Let's go out on the terrace.

(**STEVEN** *hesitates.*)

Humor me.

(*He sighs, takes hold of* **MARJORIE**'s *chair.*)

MARY. (*Wheeling* **ROSE** *out of the room.*) Did Rosie forget to go potty before her nap?

(*The focus shifts to the terrace.* **STEVEN** *pushes* **MARJORIE** *to the center.*)

STEVEN. I think you'll like your room.

(*Pause.*)

Bright, sunny.

(*Pause.*)

You'll be sharing it with a Mrs. Murphy. I wanted you to have a private room, but the nurse said it would be easier for you to adjust if you had a roommate. I think you'll like Mrs. Murphy. She seems to keep to herself.

MARJORIE. All right. I'll agree to a few days. Till I'm back on my feet.

STEVEN. Mother, you've been sick for a long time now. More than a month, and well, things just don't stand still.

MARJORIE. I realize that; if I'm behind on a few bills...

STEVEN. I've taken care of the bills. But there were decisions to be made. In the last two years you've gone through almost thirty percent of Dad's estate.

MARJORIE. I've been redecorating.

STEVEN. That's another thing. What you've done to the house. There was nothing wrong with it.

MARJORIE. It was pretentious. And stuffy. It's always been stuffy.

STEVEN. You painted latex over gold leaf wall coverings!

MARJORIE. I should have done it years ago. Maybe there would have been some joy in that house if it had been brighter.

STEVEN. To say nothing of practically giving away the antiques.

MARJORIE. Steven, when you get as old as me, you begin losing your reverence for age.

> *(Holding out her hand.)*

Come here.

> *(He goes to her, she takes his hand.)*

This isn't you talking. You've never been greedy. It's your brother and sister, isn't it? Don't let them use you, Steven. Don't destroy the special closeness you and I have had. Remember when you were in college and you used to sneak home Saturday mornings and we'd sit in the kitchen over a pot of tea and talk for hours and hours? I miss those times. I want you to promise me something. When I get home –

> *(**STEVEN** pulls away.)*

What's wrong?

STEVEN. This is your home, now.

MARJORIE. I mean later, after I've recovered.

STEVEN. It was a sixteen room house, Mother. The maintenance, utilities, taxes. We had no other choice.

MARJORIE. Choice. About what!

STEVEN. It wasn't safe for you to be there all alone. Look at you, how can you possibly –

MARJORIE. If you've done anything with my house, I swear to god –

STEVEN. I told you, we had to make some decisions. We had an offer.

MARJORIE. IT'S NOT FOR SALE!

STEVEN. And we accepted.

MARJORIE. NO!

STEVEN. Michael signed the contract at ten o'clock Friday morning. The house has been sold.

MARJORIE. *(Beginning to seethe.)* He's not going to get away with this. Michael had no right. I'm calling Harry Elkind –

STEVEN. Harry Elkind is Michael's attorney, too. While you were in the hospital they petitioned the court to declare you incompetent. As the oldest Michael was appointed conservator.

MARJORIE. Incompetent!

STEVEN. You were unconscious, we didn't know if you were going to live or die!

MARJORIE. Couldn't you have waited? Or were you that anxious to divvy up the spoils!

STEVEN. Do you think I want this? I was elected to bring you here because I'm Mother's favorite, her baby. All I can say is be thankful it's me. Michael and Diane, they would have sent you here in a cab.

MARJORIE. Yes, thank you.

STEVEN. Oh, Mom.

(He walks to the railing.)

You know I'd love to ask you to come home with me. But you and Patsy have never gotten along. And the girls, what can I say, they're teenagers. Mom, I've been driving myself crazy with this thing; over and over it a thousand times. This is the best I can do.

(Quiet pause.)

I put everything from the house in storage. They told me you can have a few personal things here in your room. Small things. Just let me know. And if you need money – Michael thought it would be best if he transferred your checking and savings accounts into a special account which he'll administer. But he told me to tell you if you need money for anything, anything at all, just call him.

*(**MARY** returns with **ROSE** to the rec room.)*

There's some saliva dripping from your mouth. Here, let me –

*(He takes a handkerchief, bends down, **MARJORIE** slaps him in the face.)*

MARY. *(Entering the terrace.)* Mr. Kendrick? Excuse me, but I think we should get your mother settled.

STEVEN. Is there anything you can do for her?

MARY. Of course.

(She takes a packet of pills from her pocket.)

Here we go, Marjorie. These will make you feel better.

*(She puts the pills in **MARJORIE**'s hand and pours her a glass of water.)*

Come on. Swallow them down. Doctor's orders.

*(**MARJORIE** throws the pills into **MARY**'s face.)*

STEVEN. I think I had better go.

MARY. That might be best.

STEVEN. Just give it a chance, okay? I've been up and down Long Island. Checked out more than a dozen nursing homes and this was the best. A resort, that's what it is.

(*He kisses her on her left cheek and exits.*)

MARY. He seems like a nice boy. Are you warm enough? Here, why don't we button –

MARJORIE. Get your hands off me.

MARY. Marjorie. I know what you're going through, I really do. And I'll spend all the time I can with you, but I've also got twenty-two people to take care of in this quad. Many have no bladder or bowel control, many can't feed, wash or clothe themselves. And we're shorthanded. I know a sudden adjustment like this, it's hard, but it will be much easier if you try to think about other people as well as yourself.

MARJORIE. I spent my entire life thinking of other people. Finally, when I get a chance...

MARY. (*Pouring a glass of water.*) The welcome packet on your bedstand explains the policies and procedures here at Sunset Terrace. Once you've gone over them I'd be happy to answer any questions. We want you to be happy here, Marjorie. We really do.

(*Offering* **MARJORIE** *a small cup with pills and the glass of water.*)

Here. These will help, they really will.

(**MARJORIE** *stares at the cup a moment then washes them down.*)

That's fine.

(A bell rings. **MARY** *sighs.)*

No rest for the weary.

(Pushing **MARJORIE**'s *wheelchair.)*

Why don't you wait in here with Henry and Rose. I'll be right back in a moment to take you to your room.

(She pushes **MARJORIE** *to the table and exits.)*

HENRY. So how did it go?

MARJORIE. *(Stiffening.)* Fine.

HENRY. Good.

(They sit there a moment.)

Seems like a nice boy. Steven.

MARJORIE. *(Starting to cry.)* I shouldn't have slapped him. It's not his fault. The others, they put him up to it. They treat me as if – their father was the same way – as if –

(Stifling the tears.)

I'm sorry. You told me you like to stay out of other people's affairs.

HENRY. It's okay.

MARJORIE. No.

HENRY. Really. My mother always wanted me to be a priest.

MARJORIE. From priesthood to convict. That's quite a leap.

(Opening her hand, revealing two pills.)

Will you tell me something? These pills, do you know what they are?

HENRY. Where'd you get them?

MARJORIE. The nurse just now. I pretended to take them.

HENRY. Pretended?

MARJORIE. I don't take drugs unless I know what they're for.

HENRY. No, I – I don't know what they are.

MARJORIE. Is there any way I can find out?

HENRY. Marge, you're going to get into trouble.

MARJORIE. Worse trouble than being here?

HENRY. It can get worse, and that's all I'm going to say.

MARJORIE. They're tranquilizers, aren't they?

HENRY. It's none of my business. Yours either.

MARJORIE. Of course it's my business. She can't just reach into her pocket and –

HENRY. Did you see yourself when your son left? Mary was doing you a favor. Come on now, try and see the bright side.

MARJORIE. What bright side?

HENRY. I don't know. How about there's tears coming out both your eyes?

(*Looks closer.*)

Yep, both of them. Look, Rose, Marjorie's getting better.

ROSE. Oh, my.

(**MARJORIE** *looks at her two companions, laughs a moment, then continues to cry.*)

Scene Two

(Three weeks later. **ISABEL**, **HENRY**, **ABE**, **ROSE** *and* **DOTTIE** *are sitting on the terrace.* **DOTTIE**, **ISABEL** *and* **ROSE** *are asleep.)*

ABE. Look at this. A letter from my wife. She's flying the Concord to Paris. Me, I'm stuck on the commode all day and she's flying the Concord to Paris.

HENRY. That's what you get for marrying a woman twenty years younger than you.

ABE. You make it sound like I married a teenager. She's forty-one years old. You've seen her. I married her out of sympathy, and look how she shows her gratitude. Just because I've got a slight colon infection. I told her, "Joellen," I said, "I got a bathroom at home. I got a bathroom in my office. And on the subway in between who's going to notice?"

HENRY. It's getting worse, isn't it?

ABE. You noticed.

HENRY. Hard not to.

ABE. I'm starting to think it might be something more serious. I mean the pills they give me aren't helping at all.

HENRY. You talked to your doctor?

ABE. Son–of–a–bitch. Promised he'd be here the last four Wednesdays in a row. Every time he's canceled.

HENRY. Know what your problem is? You won't accept the fact you're growing old.

ABE. Damn right I won't accept it. Old age is cruel and sadistic and I intend to fight it every step of the way!

HENRY. Good for you. I admire a man with uncontrollable diarrhea who has the courage to shout, "I won't take this sitting down!"

*(**MARY** wheels **MARJORIE** through the double doors of the recreation room. **MARJORIE** is now in nightgown and robe. Her hair is a mess.)*

MARJORIE. I tell you, my roommate is dead.

MARY. Now, Marjorie.

MARJORIE. She is! I've been watching her for three weeks and she hasn't so much as batted an eyelash.

MARY. Mrs. Murphy is fine.

MARJORIE. Yesterday I held a mirror to her face. Not a breath. I shouted into her ear. Not a flinch. This morning I stuck her with a pin. She didn't even bleed.

MARY. I wish you'd stop pestering poor Mrs. Murphy.

MARJORIE. I tried to pick up her arm. It was stiff as a board.

MARY. She has arthritis.

MARJORIE. She has rigor mortis. My son told me she keeps to herself. Show me a dead woman that doesn't keep to herself!

MARY. *(Pushing **MARJORIE** on to the terrace.)* Here we all are. Enjoying the afternoon sun.

HENRY. That you, Marge? Where you been all morning?

MARJORIE. My doctor came to visit me.

ABE. Listen to that. She's here only three weeks and already a visit from her doctor.

HENRY. What did he say, Marge?

MARY. *(To **HENRY**.)* Tell Henry what your doctor said, Marjorie. He scolded her for not showing more improvement.

MARJORIE. Why don't you mind your own business.

MARY. Everyone wait here. I'll be back in a minute with the lunch trays.

(She exits.)

ABE. Don't hurry.

HENRY. Is it true, Marge? You're not getting any better?

MARJORIE. I asked my doctor about those pills, Henry. They are tranquilizers. Double strength.

ABE. What pills?

MARJORIE. Same thing you're taking, Abe. In fact nearly everyone here gets three or four of them a day. Explains why you all sit around like zombies.

HENRY. Marge, what you do to yourself is one thing, but you've no right to meddle –

ABE. Why would they be giving me tranquilizers?

MARJORIE. When I asked the doctor he patted my hand and said, "Be a good girl, Marjorie, take your pills."

HENRY. You shouldn't listen to her, Abe.

MARJORIE. And that's just one of the things we take. Look at the pill cart when Mary comes back. Some of those cups look like they're filled with confetti.

HENRY. *(Standing.)* I'm not listening to this.

ABE. Just a minute, Henry. We've got a right to know what medicine we're taking.

HENRY. Abe, you've been here long enough to know what this kind of talk will get us.

MARJORIE. I think I know a way we can find out. There's a book in the nurses station. I noticed it last week. A pharmaceutical directory. Henry, if you could just –

HENRY. Me?

MARJORIE. Well I can't do it.

ABE. Henry, this is important.

HENRY. Even if I said yes, which I won't, how do you propose I do it without getting caught?

MARJORIE. You spent eight years in a federal prison, you must have learned something.

(**MARY** *enters the recreation room pushing a cart with the lunch trays and the pills.*)

MARY. Here we are.

HENRY. *(Whispering.)* The answer's no.

MARJORIE. But you can't just...

HENRY. Yes, I can.

MARY. *(Entering the patio.)* Come on, everybody. Wake up. It's lunchtime.

ISABEL. The medications. Did you bring the medications?

MARY. Here you are, Isabel.

(*She begins passing around the paper pill cups.*)

Be careful with this, Rose. I've cleaned up enough messes for one day.

ROSE. Oh, my.

MARY. *(Giving* **ABE** *his pills.)* Abe.

(*He looks into the cup.*)

Come on, Abe, swallow them down, then help yourself to a lunch tray. Here you are, Marjorie.

DOTTIE. *(Waking up.)* What time is it?

MARY. It's time for lunch. And here's your pills.

ABE. *(Taking a lunch tray from the cart.)* They call this stuff food. They should put warning labels on these trays same as cigarettes.

(He stiffens.)

Oh no!

(He throws the tray back down on the cart.)

MARY. Abe, what's the matter?

ABE. *(Rushing out.)* What the hell do you think?

MARY. Everyone finish your lunch.

*(She hurries out after **ABE**.)*

ISABEL. *(Setting her tray aside.)* Well, any appetite we might have had – Feel like a game of poker, Henry?

HENRY. Maybe later.

ISABEL. Come on, Rose. Let's go in and watch TV.

*(**ROSE** keeps eating as **ISABEL** pushes her out.)*

DOTTIE. *(Getting up.)* Henry, may I borrow a quarter for the pay phone?

HENRY. On the dresser in my room.

*(**HENRY** gets up and goes behind Marge's chair.)*

DOTTIE. *(Exiting.)* Such a bright, sunny day.

HENRY. Marge? Want me to push you inside?

MARJORIE. No.

HENRY. Soaps are on.

MARJORIE. I'd just as soon stay here.

*(**HENRY** turns to go back inside, stops, turns back.)*

HENRY. You keep this up you're going to get us all into trouble. It's an adjustment moving here, I realize that, but with a little patience –

MARJORIE. *(Snapping.)* Patience is only a virtue when you're waiting for something besides death!

(She tries to open her cosmetic bag.)

Here, help me with this.

(**HENRY** *opens it for her.*)

HENRY. What are you doing?

MARJORIE. Nothing.

HENRY. What did you put in that bag?

MARJORIE. What do you think?

HENRY. I'm warning you.

MARJORIE. Like you warned Isabel?

HENRY. Isabel? What's she got to do with this?

MARJORIE. Come off it, Henry. You're not so blind that you can't see Isabel's hooked on these things.

HENRY. I don't know what you're talking about.

MARJORIE. I thought you cared about Isabel!

HENRY. *(Going to the railing.)* It's none of my business! Yours either!

(Pause.)

If Isabel had listened to me – All that was wrong with her when she first came here was a broken hip. But she was feisty. Wouldn't obey the rules. So they started mixing tranquilizers with her painkillers. And now? Yeah, she's addicted to them.

MARJORIE. They did this to her deliberately?

HENRY. It's economics, Marge. This place exists for one reason. To make a buck. Which means they'll save money any way they can. Like they're always saying they're shorthanded. Hell, they've been shorthanded since the day I got here. Why hire a nurse's aide when one little pill can do the job for a fraction of the cost.

MARJORIE. But what about the doctors? Why do they permit this?

HENRY. Doctors. You know what Sunset Terrace is to them? It's a reminder that someday these warriors against death are going to lose. They'll do anything to avoid this place. Like write any prescription the nurses want. And they add "PRN" to the charts. Know what that means? "As often as needed." The nurses here have a license to feed you as many pills as they want.

MARJORIE. That can't be true.

HENRY. It is. And don't be too shocked because it's probably on your chart as well. "PRN" right up on top. Often as needed.

MARJORIE. How do you know all this?

HENRY. I did learn things in prison. Survival skills.

MARJORIE. So I'm supposed to sit here and be a good little girl. No fuss, no demands. Sit here like Rose and not even bother them when I have to urinate?

HENRY. All I'm saying is go along with things. A few pills won't hurt you. It's when you make trouble, that's when they start to double and triple the doses.

MARJORIE. Not me, buster. Every pill they give me's going right into my little bag.

HENRY. They'll find out. And when they do they'll inject the stuff into you. You can't win, Marge. I've been here a long time and I've seen it happen. Why do you think they don't give me any of that stuff. It's because I cooperate.

MARJORIE. One of your survival skills.

HENRY. I'm still here.

MARJORIE. Big deal. You survive. Damnit, Henry, there's more to life than just getting by.

HENRY. Oh, what's the point in talking to you? I guess what they say about old dogs is true.

MARJORIE. An old dog, am I? Pardon me for saying this, Henry, but do you know what you are? You're a lump. A certified, professional, major league lump.

HENRY. Is that right?

MARJORIE. That's right.

HENRY. Well, pardon me for saying this, Marjorie, but you're a trouble maker.

MARJORIE. Well, I'd rather be making something, even if it's only trouble, than just sitting on my duff taking up space.

HENRY. At least I know my place.

MARJORIE. It's no wonder, you've been glued to it for seventy years.

HENRY. Is that right?

MARJORIE. That's right!

HENRY. At least I don't go around stirring things up with a lot of hot air. A big, puffy bag of it. It's a wonder you don't float away like a balloon. I know your type, Marge. I've known your type for fifty years. Sylvia. She was another one.

MARJORIE. Sylvia?

HENRY. Promised she'd wait. Swore she'd be faithful.

MARJORIE. You expected Sylvia to wait until you got out of prison?

HENRY. She promised!

MARJORIE. Eight years?

HENRY. I'd have waited!

MARJORIE. THAT'S BECAUSE YOU'RE A LUMP!

HENRY. IS THAT RIGHT?

MARJORIE. THAT'S RIGHT!

> *(They turn away from each other and sit quietly fuming for a few moments.* **MARJORIE** *mellows quickly and starts to chuckle.)*

HENRY. What are you laughing at?

MARJORIE. I'm not sure.

HENRY. Our first fight. Know something? We must be developing a relationship.

MARJORIE. Carter and I used to fight a lot. Not like this. Bitter, mean fights. Last for days. I met him during the war. At the USO off Times Square. Lieutenant Carter Monroe Kendrick. We had a two-week whirlwind romance. Finest restaurants, theatres, nightclubs. He told me he was being shipped off to France. Asked me to marry him. So many of us at that time. Thought it was our patriotic duty. Give the boys something to come home to. So I said, yes. Spent a weekend in the honeymoon suite at the Plaza. Me. I thought I had stumbled into an F. Scott Fitzgerald novel. Then he was gone.

HENRY. How long was he in France?

MARJORIE. France? Ha! I didn't hear from him for four months. Then one day I get a call from his mother. Would I meet her for lunch? Turns out Carter had a cushy job as a procurement officer and was stationed all along at West Point. The only action that boy ever saw during the war was when he showed up for his little Midtown flings. But he was a moral boy. Wouldn't go to bed with a woman unless he was married to her. Seems I was the third Mrs. David Kendrick in as many years. His mother asked if I'd agree to a settlement. I said, gladly. Except I happened to be four months pregnant. So I moved to Westhampton. Lived with David forty years in perfect misery. Doesn't seem fair, does it?

HENRY. Don't tell me, Marge. Know all about it. Lust can do that to you.

MARJORIE. Lust?

HENRY. What happened between me and Sylvia, you and David. That's all it was, pure and unadulterated lust.

MARJORIE. What are you talking about? Lust. We were young. Simple biological drives. No different than hungering for a hot pastrami on rye.

HENRY. Oh, yeah? Well my hot pastrami on rye got me eight years behind bars. A hot pastrami, by the way, that I never even tasted.

MARJORIE. You mean you and Sylvia never –

HENRY. All she kept saying was, "Not until we're married." Maybe that's why I expected her to wait. She owed me! Back there in Otisville I vowed that lust would never get the better of me again. And I've kept that vow.

MARJORIE. You don't mean –

HENRY. I'm not a pervert, if that's what you're thinking. A great many perfectly healthy men I mean there have been popes and priests and –

MARJORIE. Are you saying that you've never –

HENRY. Prison life offered lots of alternatives, let me tell you. But I didn't go in for that sort of thing. No matter how difficult it got.

MARJORIE. Then you've never I mean not once ever done –

HENRY. It?

MARJORIE. It.

HENRY. Not something I planned. Does it make a difference?

MARJORIE. Oh, no. Of course not. After you got out. Of prison. What did you –

HENRY. Went home. Back to Queens. My mother had arranged a job for me at Our Lady of Sorrows. Custodian? I was serious when I said she wanted me to become a priest. But this was as close as I could get. She'd come by afternoons, sit in the back of the church. Watch me clean the altar.

(They sit quietly for a moment.)

MARJORIE. Don't you still have...I mean urges?

HENRY. Urges?

MARJORIE. The...hots.

HENRY. I told you I was a normal man. 'Course I have urges. Sometimes. Wouldn't call them the "hots" anymore. More like the "lukewarms."

MARJORIE. Don't get me wrong. I'm no expert on the subject. Carter, he was the only one I ever had –

HENRY. It.

MARJORIE. – with, yes. He was such a businessman. Even in bed. He'd make an appointment with me days in advance. And when the time arrived it would be quick, efficient. I think he would have been pleased if at the end of the month I'd have sent him a statement. I've read a lot of novels. The things women experience. I never, with Carter, I mean, you know, had a – an –

(She slams her hand down on her chair.)

Why is this so difficult to talk about! I'm an emerging widow, damnit! Orgasm! There, I've said it! And not only that, Henry, I've played with myself!

HENRY. OH MY GOD!

MARJORIE. Why are you so shocked? Surely, you must have – Don't tell me you've never – I mean even your popes and priests –

HENRY. I didn't say I never. What do you think I did with my urges!

MARJORIE. Henry, there's something I want to talk to you about.

HENRY. THE ANSWER'S NO!

(*He gets up.*)

I'm going in and watching TV. Though god knows, the soap operas'll be *Sesame Street* after this.

MARJORIE. No, Henry, wait.

(*He stops.*)

That subject's closed, okay? There's something else. Please? I realize you don't think we can change much around here. And you're probably right. That's why I've been thinking about – running away. No, no. Relax. Look at me, how far would I get? Be the same as if you tried it. But what about two people who separately might not have all their faculties, but together – I mean you have a strong pair of legs, strong arms. And me, my eyesight is near perfect, my hearing. What I'm trying to say is, what if we pooled our resources, why couldn't we –

HENRY. What?

MARJORIE. Leave here.

HENRY. Leave?

MARJORIE. Find a place of our own.

HENRY. You and me?

MARJORIE. Yes.

HENRY. Together?

MARJORIE. Does it sound that crazy?

HENRY. For godsake, Marge, we've only known each other three weeks!

MARJORIE. What do you want, a formal courtship? Your eyes and ears are almost gone, Henry. How long can the rest last? Don't say no, right away. Think about it, okay? Just think about it?

(*They sit quietly for a moment.*)

Would you – hold my hand?

(*Slowly he reaches out.*)

No, this hand.

HENRY. But that's your –

MARJORIE. I can close it now.

(*He takes her left hand.*)

See. If I concentrate real hard I can close it.

HENRY. Very firm.

MARJORIE. This is nice.

(*Pause.*)

You're hand is warm.

(**ISABEL** *calls out from the other room.*)

ISABEL. Henry, feel like a game now?

HENRY. Let go, Marge. The others, they're going to see.

ISABEL. Henry!

HENRY. Marge!

MARJORIE. I'm trying, Henry.

HENRY. No, you're squeezing tighter. The other way!

(**MARJORIE** *starts laughing.*)

You're doing this on purpose.

MARJORIE. No, I'm trying. I get mixed up.

ISABEL. What are you two doing out there?

HENRY. I'll pull it out. Hold on to your chair. Ready?

> (**HENRY** *jerks and as he does he pulls* **MARJORIE** *to a standing position. She screams then roars with laughter.*)

Now look what you've gone and done!

MARJORIE. Look at me! Oops. Catch me, Henry!

HENRY. *(His arms go around her, holding her up.)* How the hell am I going to get you back in that chair?

MARJORIE. What's your hurry? Oh, it feels so good to be taller than the doorknobs!

HENRY. I've got a hernia, you know.

MARJORIE. Poor Henry.

> (**MARY** *enters the rec room. Hears the commotion out on the terrace, heads that way.*)

HENRY. Now cut that out!

MARJORIE. Lighten up, Henry. Come on. We can "emerge" together.

HENRY. Your chair keeps rolling away. Do something. Lock the brakes.

MARJORIE. Whee! This is almost like dancing.

> (**MARY** *enters the terrace. Stops.* **HENRY** *sees her, but* **MARJORIE** *doesn't.*)

Mmm. You smell good. You smell like a man.

> *(She tries to kiss him.)*

HENRY. Marge!

MARJORIE. Tell me more about your lukewarms. Does it happen in the morning when nurse Mary gives you your bath?

HENRY. For godsakes, Marge, look –

MARJORIE. Of course, Nurse Mueller isn't a very good example. Her face would make the Washington monument go limp.

MARY. You two having fun? I'm surprised at you, Henry. You used to be a model patient. But perhaps it wasn't your fault. You can let go, I have her.

MARJORIE. You're hurting me.

MARY. *(She helps* **MARJORIE** *back into her chair.)* Now Marjorie, I told you we're short handed. This kind of childish behavior –

MARJORIE. Childish. We were simply –

HENRY. It wasn't Marge's fault. She sort of fell out of her chair.

MARY. Fell out of her chair? Good heavens, why didn't you say so?

MARJORIE. I didn't fall out, I –

MARY. Don't be embarrassed, Marjorie. It's a common problem. These chairs aren't the steadiest things.

MARJORIE. No, they're not, but –

MARY. Fortunately, we have a very simple solution.

> *(***MARY*** pulls two white strips of cotton cloth from her pocket.)*

MARJORIE. What are you doing?

> *(***MARY*** ties* **MARJORIE***'s wrists to the arms of the chair.)*

MARY. Can't have you falling out of your chair, now can we?

MARJORIE. This is outrageous! I didn't fall out of my chair. Tell her, Henry. Tell her what happened!

MARY. Now settle down. Let's see if a few days like this helps you with your...equilibrium.

(*A bell rings.* **MARY** *sighs.*)

No rest for the weary.

(**MARY** *goes off.* **MARJORIE** *and* **HENRY** *sit quietly for a moment.*)

MARJORIE. Untie me, Henry.

HENRY. I warned you, Marge. Didn't I warn you?

MARJORIE. Untie me!

HENRY. (*Struggles with it a moment.*) I've gotten along all this time on a couple of simple rules. Keep my nose out of other people's business and do what I'm told.

(**DOTTIE** *enters the terrace followed by* **ISABEL** *who is pushing* **ROSE** *in her chair.*)

ISABEL. What's all the commotion out here? Mueller steamed by like an old locomotive.

DOTTIE. (*To* **MARJORIE**.) And look at you. When did you get tied up like that?

MARJORIE. The nurse.

DOTTIE. Mary? She did that to you? Why?

MARJORIE. I tried to give Henry a kiss.

ISABEL. Henry? That ugly thing? I don't blame her for tying you up.

MARJORIE. Untie me. Please. Isabel?

(**ISABEL** *doesn't move.*)

Dottie?

(No one moves.)

What on earth is wrong with all of you? You're right, Henry. It was stupid of me to think any of us will ever get out of here.

DOTTIE. I'm getting out of here. Nancy's coming to get me tomorrow.

MARJORIE. Oh, Dottie, for the love of god, when are you going to accept the fact that Nancy is not coming for you!

HENRY. Marge!

DOTTIE. You don't know what you're talking about. Isabel, tell her she doesn't know what she's talking about.

ISABEL. You shouldn't say things like that, Marjorie. Dottie's very sensitive.

DOTTIE. I just talked to Nancy this morning. She said she – She did. She said –

HENRY. Maybe her daughter will come. How do you know?

ISABEL. Look, you made her cry. Now, now, Dottie. Marjorie didn't mean what she said.

HENRY. Nancy's coming, Dottie. Maybe even tomorrow, if it's sunny.

MARJORIE. I'm sorry, Dottie. Forgive me. I didn't mean –

ISABEL. What started this, anyway?

HENRY. Marge thinks if we "pooled our resources" we could break out of here.

ISABEL. You mean run away? All of us? At the same time?

MARJORIE. I wasn't thinking grand scale, but – why not?

*(**ABE** walks on to the terrace.)*

ISABEL. Abe. You should hear this.

DOTTIE. Marjorie doesn't think Nancy's going to come get me.

ISABEL. She also has the absurd idea –

MARJORIE. Abe, would you please come over here and untie me?

ABE. *(Crossing to* **MARJORIE.***)* How did this happen?

DOTTIE. Mary caught Marjorie trying to give Henry a kiss.

MARJORIE. Please, Abe.

ABE. What's it worth to you? Maybe I should get a kiss, too?

> *(***MARJORIE** *slumps in her chair.)*

Nevermind. I'll untie you for nothing.

HENRY. *(Grabs* **ABE.** *Turns him around.)* Don't be a damned fool!

ABE. Too late, Henry, I'm already a damned fool. Look at this.

> *(He pulls a large book from under his sweater.)*

ISABEL. What on earth –

ABE. It's that pharmacy guide. See. It's got pictures and descriptions of every pill made today. Couldn't wait for you, Henry. I went and swiped it myself.

HENRY. Have you lost your mind!

ABE. You were right, Marjorie.

> *(Puts the book on the table in front of* **MARJORIE.***)*

They have been giving me tranquilizers. Heavy duty tranquilizers. That's not all. Here, let's sit down.

> *(They all sit.* **ABE** *opens the book.)*

You remember, Henry, I came here with a colon infection. Couldn't control myself. Doctor told me I'd be out in a couple of weeks. The first pill they give me was this one. Page sixty-seven. An antibiotic. Look at the side effects. Stomach upset. That's what happened to me. So they gave me this pill. Page fifty-three. A digestive aid. But it made me dizzy. So they gave me this pill. Page twenty-eight. A dopamine inhibitor. But that made me drowsy. So they gave me this pill. A psychotropic. I get three of them a day every day. You'll never guess one of the side effects.

(He pushes the book in front of **MARJORIE** *and points to spot on the page.)*

MARJORIE. Oh, good god.

HENRY. What? What is it?

MARJORIE. *(Looking up.)* It can cause severe diarrhea.

ABE. These sonsabitches have been keeping me going for nine months!

HENRY. They didn't do it deliberately.

ABE. Maybe not, but it's at least medical negligence.

ISABEL. I can't believe your doctor wouldn't have known.

ABE. Look for yourself. And while you're at it, Isabel, look up those little yellow pills you're so fond of.

HENRY. *(Grabbing the book.)* Give me that! This whole damn thing has gone far enough! Look what you've done, Marjorie. You were right. You should get out of here. Leave the rest of us in peace!

ABE. Get out of here? What are you talking about?

DOTTIE. Marjorie wants us all to run away.

MARJORIE. No. Just me. The rest of you can stay here and rot!

(She struggles with her chair.)

ABE. Wait, I'm going with you!

HENRY. Abe, be serious!

ABE. Serious? Take one last look at me, Henry, cause you're never going to see anyone more serious in your life! Come on, Marjorie!

DOTTIE. You're leaving? You really mean it?

HENRY. And where you going to go? Tell me that.

MARJORIE. We'll find a place.

ABE. That's right. A place of our own.

DOTTIE. You mean like a house?

MARJORIE. A house, an apartment, a tar paper shack. Anything'd be better than here.

DOTTIE. A house would be nice. I could get my things. Albert's and my things.

HENRY. Dottie, for godsake, I thought Nancy was coming to get you tomorrow?

DOTTIE. I can wait for Nancy in a house with my things as easy as I can wait here!

ISABEL. What'll you use for money? You can't just –

MARJORIE. I'm sure if we pooled our social security –

DOTTIE. Even a little house.

ISABEL. You know what's going to happen, don't you? You two take off and they'll blame us for it.

DOTTIE. I have laces and linens. They've been sitting in boxes for years.

ISABEL. You're not leaving me behind to take the rap.

MARJORIE. Then come with us!

HENRY. Listen to me! You're all talking stupid!

MARJORIE. Stupid? Put us all together, Henry. The talent, the skills, the experience we possess, it's mind boggling! I mean, my god, we've all lived through a depression, umpteen wars and – and The Beatles!

ABE. You give me one good reason for staying here, Henry, one good reason and I'll do it!

MARY. *(Entering the rec room briskly.)* Attention, everyone!

(**ABE** *grabs the pill book and shoves it under Rose's lap blanket.* **MARY** *enters the terrace.*)

I have some wonderful news. Mrs. Lundsford from the Craft Guild is coming this afternoon to show us all how to make paper flowers!

(Everyone looks at her blankly.)

I knew you'd be excited. Three-thirty. Here in the recreation room. Don't be late.

(She exits.)

ABE. That it, Henry? You hung up on paper flowers!

MARJORIE. Or ceramic ashtrays!

DOTTIE. Or paint-by-numbers!

ISABEL. You got to admit it, Henry. The thought of nobody waking you at five in the morning to stick an enema up your butt is pretty appealing.

MARJORIE. Or pinching you, pushing you, herding you from room to room like cattle.

ABE. We could celebrate the Holy Days.

DOTTIE. Like Christmas.

ABE. Hanukkah, you old bat!

MARJORIE. Maybe we could find a house with a fireplace. Can you imagine it, Henry. Some winter night, snuggling on a sofa in front of a warm, romantic fire?

ABE. Smoking a two dollar cigar.

DOTTIE. Sipping a glass of warm brandy.

HENRY. It's a pretty dream. It is. Like I asked before, where would we go?

MARJORIE. We'll find a house, Henry. I know we will!

HENRY. WHERE!

ROSE. *(Without looking up.)* I – have one.

DOTTIE. Rose, did you say something?

ROSE. Oh, my.

> *(**ROSE** looks down.)*

DOTTIE. You have one. What, honey? What is it you have?

> *(**ROSE** doesn't look up.)*

Rose?

ROSE. I have –

ISABEL. Yes?

ROSE. House.

ABE. What?

ROSE. House. Big house. Raised six kids in it. They're all gone. Just sitting there. The house. Empty.

> *(They all stare at **ROSE** for a moment.)*

ABE. You're serious.

ROSE. I have pictures. In my room. 527 North Tyler. You're all welcome to – I mean...

MARJORIE. What? Rose?

ROSE. You would take me with you, wouldn't you?

ISABEL. Oh my god. We really can do it.

HENRY. Now just a minute, just a – Something like this. It would take weeks, of – of planning. I mean –

MARJORIE. You're right, Henry. We should plan.

ABE. And we can start by identifying all the pills. Sort out the ones we need to take from the ones they want us to take.

MARJORIE. We've got to be careful, Abe.

ABE. Careful. I'm an expert on being careful. I don't even sneeze without being careful.

(Grabbing the book.)

Come on, everybody. Let's go back inside and get to work.

(They start to leave.)

DOTTIE. This is all so exciting.

ISABEL. Terrifying, you mean.

HENRY. I still think –

MARJORIE. Wait!

ABE. What's the matter?

MARJORIE. What's the matter? Untie me, goddamnit!

(Everyone hesitates a moment. Finally **HENRY** *shrugs, goes to* **MARJORIE** *and begins to remove her restraints.)*

ACT II

(The recreation room a week later. It's evening, and the room has a warm glow. **HENRY** *is at the record player; everyone else is at the table playing cards.)*

HENRY. *(Putting a record on the machine.)* How's this one?

(The music begins.*)

Recognize it?

MARJORIE. Yes.

ABE. Feeling a little romantic tonight, Henry?

DOTTIE. Albert and I used to go listen to Paul Whiteman on the roof of the Biltmore. That must be fifty years ago. And we danced. I've never danced with a man who could dance like Albert. Do you dance, Henry?

HENRY. Me? No.

ISABEL. Come on, Dottie, it's your play. Cost you fifty bucks to stay in the game.

DOTTIE. *(Throwing down her cards.)* Oh, I'm tired of this. I hope when we move we don't sit around all day playing cards. Abe, you don't dance, do you?

ABE. Dance? I taught Arthur Murray how to dance.

---

* A license to produce *Last Resort* does not include a performance license for any third-party or copyrighted music. Licensees should create an original composition or use music in the public domain. For further information, please see the Music and Third-Party Materials Use Note on page iii.

DOTTIE. Really?

> *(She bats her eyelashes at him.)*

ABE. What is this? They put something in the water?

MARJORIE. Come on, Abe, dance with her.

ABE. Did I say I wouldn't?

DOTTIE. You mean you will?

ABE. *(Going up to* **DOTTIE**, *bowing slightly.)* Mrs. Bartel?

> **(DOTTIE** *gets up, curtsies. The two of them start slowly at first then gradually pickup the pace and complexity.)*

ISABEL. Look at them. Gene Kelly and Cyd Charise.

MARJORIE. Fred Astaire and Ginger Rodgers.

HENRY. Bud Abbott and Lou Costello.

ABE. Don't pay any attention to them. You're very good, Mrs. Bartel.

DOTTIE. Thank you, Mr. Waxman. You're very good yourself.

ABE. I didn't think you Catholics were allowed to dance.

DOTTIE. Of course we're allowed to dance. The Catholic religion has always been very liberal that way.

ABE. I remember when you couldn't eat meat on Friday.

DOTTIE. No, but we could eat pork chops Saturday through Thursday. I thought you Jewish men only danced with other Jewish men.

ABE. That's only when our wives are around.

DOTTIE. Did you dance much with your wife?

ABE. Only once. I've been wearing Dr. Schols ever since.

MARJORIE. Aren't they wonderful?

(**ABE** *and* **DOTTIE** *do a complicated turn.*
ROSE *applauds.*)

HENRY. I hope Abe doesn't pop his diaper pins.

(*As the music finishes the two dancers end
with a flourish. Everyone applauds.*)

ABE. Thank you, Mrs. Bartel. That was most enjoyable.

DOTTIE. I'm out of breath.

(*Sitting.*)

I didn't think I'd ever dance like that again. I hope we
can keep dancing, Abe. I mean after we move.

ABE. (*To* **DOTTIE**.) Why wait? Maybe I could stop by your
room, tonight, Dottie for a little – cheek to cheek?

DOTTIE. Mr. Waxman, I hope you're not suggesting –

ABE. Don't worry. I've had a vasectomy.

ISABEL. What would your wife say if she could hear you talk?

ABE. You think Joellen's so innocent? Flying all over the
world? She called me yesterday from Rio to find out
what I wanted for my birthday. You know what I told
her? Revenge.

HENRY. What's Joellen going to say when she finds out
you've left Sunset Terrace?

ABE. Who cares. I wouldn't be surprised if this whole
diarrhea thing was her idea.

ISABEL. We still haven't decided who's going to be in charge.

HENRY. I still think it should be Marjorie. This was her idea.

ABE. Yes, but it's Rose's house.

DOTTIE. I'd like to have a man in charge.

ISABEL. Some men. Henry can barely hear or see and Abe
can't wander more than ten feet from a toilet.

MARJORIE. We've been arguing about this all week. Why do we have to have anyone in charge?

ABE. Well, someone has to be in charge. Who would we complain to?

MARJORIE. Why don't we divide the work among ourselves and let everyone be in charge of their own area. Rose, you're used to feeding a large family. What would you think about being chief cook?

ROSE. Sure, I can do that.

DOTTIE. Can I do the grocery shopping? I still have thousands of discount coupons I've saved from newspapers and magazines. I thought they were going to go to waste. Nancy doesn't believe in coupons.

HENRY. Isabel can run a gambling casino in the basement.

ABE. And if we run short of cash Henry can rob a bank.

HENRY. The sorriest day of my life, Abe Waxman, is when I told you that story.

MARJORIE. We'll need someone to take care of the laundry.

ISABEL. I can do that. As long as I can take a nap between cycles. And Marjorie, you can keep the books.

MARJORIE. If you like. So we've got the cooking, the laundry, the shopping and the books taken care of. What's left?

DOTTIE. What will we do if someone gets sick? I mean real sick.

HENRY. There's a lot of things like that we need to know.

MARJORIE. Why don't you make that your job, Henry. No one snoops better than you.

ABE. I'll do something. What can I do?

MARJORIE. What did you used to do for a living, Abe?

ABE. For a living?

HENRY. Ah ha! Now it's my turn!

ABE. Henry.

HENRY. What's the matter, Abe?

ABE. Henry, you promised.

DOTTIE. Tell us, tell us.

HENRY. He manufactured brassieres!

ROSE. Oh, my.

HENRY. That's how he met his wife. She used to model the things for catalog photographs.

MARJORIE. I thought you said your wife was plain.

ABE. We weren't photographing her face.

MARJORIE. Then we need to find a job for Abe that's "uplifting."

DOTTIE. Supportive.

ISABEL. Titillating.

ROSE. Abe could be in charge of –

(She covers her mouth and giggles.)

washing the "cups"!

ABE. I am retired from that business, so you can all stop having fun at my expense.

ISABEL. Abe's right. He's retired from that business. We need something he'd be good at now. I know.

(She bends over and whispers to the other three women. They all burst out laughing.)

ABE. What is it? What are you laughing at?

*(They whisper to **HENRY**. All laugh.)*

ABE. What is it? Come on, tell me.

THE WOMEN. *(All of them in unison.)* SANITARY ENGINEER!

ABE. Very funny.

ROSE. Speaking of that. Isabel, could you help me –

ISABEL. What is it, Rose?

ROSE. *(Embarrassed.)* Oh, my.

ISABEL. Oh. Well, of course I'll help you.

ABE. What? What's the matter?

ISABEL. *(**ROSE** stands up and with **ISABEL**'s help walks to the bathroom.)* Now you men just mind your business. When a lady has to go she has to go.

> *(Everyone applauds.)*

MARJORIE. Abe, I'll bet if Rose can learn to control it...

ABE. When you start jogging around the park, I'll throw away my diapers.

MARJORIE. I might not be able to jog yet, but I can do this.

> *(Slowly, very slowly, she picks up her left arm over her head.)*

HENRY. Marge! That's wonderful!

MARJORIE. Thank you. I can smile a whole smile now. See?

HENRY. *(Looking at her closely.)* By god, you can.

MARJORIE. I've been exercising. In my room. If I grab hold of the bed I can almost pull myself up. Give me a couple of weeks, Abe, and I'll see you in the park.

ABE. Okay, okay. When Rose gets done I'll retire to the john. I know what I can do. I'll take care of the yard. Mow the grass, prune the shrubs. How about that?

DOTTIE. *(Getting up.)* This is all so exciting. Lend me a quarter, Henry. I want to call Nancy.

ABE. Nancy?

DOTTIE. I want her to find my coupons. Oh, I won't say anything about our leaving here. I'll just tell her I need them for – I'll think of something.

HENRY. Here's a quarter, Dottie.

DOTTIE. Thank you. When we move into our new house I don't want a pay phone. I mean, I'll take care of my share of the bill, but I just think it's so degrading having to use a pay phone.

(She exits.)

HENRY. It's also mighty expensive. It's hard to believe the change in everyone in just a week. Especially Rose. I've known her for over four years and I didn't even know she could walk.

*(**ISABEL** and **ROSE** return.)*

ISABEL. Here we are.

HENRY. Your turn, Abe.

ABE. *(Getting up.)* Come on, Henry, you help me with my safety pins.

HENRY. I'll give you safety pins.

*(**ABE** goes into the bathroom.)*

ISABEL. Don't pay any attention to them, Rose. Finish what you were telling me.

ROSE. *(To **ISABEL**.)* Well, my oldest boy – he's not a boy, really, he was fifty-seven last May, he's a contractor in California. And Marcie, she's down in the Caribbean. She went there to teach and ended up marrying a local man. What Papa said about that shouldn't be repeated in mixed company. He said pretty much the same thing when Bobby went to Canada during that Viet Nam thing. And Karen's in Paris, Donald's in Greece. Says he's a philosopher but he's really a bum.

MARJORIE. You've given birth to your own United Nations.

ROSE. They're good kids. The only one who stayed home was my baby. Tommy.

MARJORIE. Do you see Tommy often?

ROSE. Oh, no. He was killed in a car accident back in 1980.

MARJORIE. I'm sorry.

ROSE. Yes. He was going to take over Papa's business. Poor Papa. He never got over his baby's death.

MARJORIE. What are your children going to think about you moving home?

ROSE. I think they'll be pleased. They never wanted me to leave in the first place. When I had my operation, Karen was going to come home from Europe and take care of me. But I couldn't let her do that. She had this fellowship, she worked hard for it and I couldn't just let her –

ABE. *(Rushing out of the bathroom.)* Everybody. Quick, come look!

ISABEL. What is it, Abe, what's happened?

ABE. It's the most beautiful thing I've ever seen. I got up from the commode, looked down, and – I thought my eyes were playing tricks on me.

HENRY. You mean –

ABE. You don't believe me, come look! It's round, it's firm, it's beautiful!

ISABEL. My god, then it was the medicine all along.

ABE. I felt like a father staring down at his firstborn.

HENRY. Maybe you should pass out cigars.

ABE. If I had them I would.

MARJORIE. Go flush the toilet, Abe.

ABE. *(Going back to the bathroom.)* Flush it? Not on your life! I'm going to have it bronzed!

ISABEL. I hope you have plenty of bathrooms in your house, Rose. May I see that picture again?

ROSE. *(Handing her a snapshot.)* I wish I had something more recent. Those maple trees, they're twice that size now. After Papa died I didn't feel much like taking pictures.

HENRY. Probably have to help Abe keep this yard up. Lot of work. Going to need a set of electric clippers. Come to think of it, is the power on at the house, Rose?

ROSE. The electricity? I don't really know.

HENRY. *(Taking out a pen and note pad.)* Give me the address again, I'll call and check.

ROSE. 527 North Tyler.

*(**DOTTIE** enters as **ABE** comes out of the bathroom.)*

DOTTIE. That girl. It's a mortal sin what's she's done.

ABE. What happened?

DOTTIE. Nancy threw them away. I had coupons for everything from acne creams to Ziploc bags.

MARJORIE. You didn't say anything about –

DOTTIE. Of course not. I told her they shouldn't go to waste.

*(**MARY** enters pushing her pill cart.)*

MARY. Well, now. Aren't we a cozy group?

(Everyone freezes.)

MARY. Am I interrupting something?

(*They all shake their heads.* **MARY** *passes out the pills.*)

Come on, swallow these down. Look at the time. I was supposed to clock out of here twenty minutes ago.

ABE. Stepping out tonight, are we, Mary?

MARY. As a matter of fact. There's a full moon this evening and I have a date.

ABE. Who are you meeting? The Wolfman?

MARY. Here Rose. Now don't spill them.

ROSE. Oh, my.

MARY. Here you go, Dottie. Nancy didn't come today, did she? Maybe tomorrow.

DOTTIE. Yes. If it's sunny.

(*She winks at* **ABE.**)

MARY. (*Giving* **MARJORIE** *her pills.*) You all certainly have been having a good time lately.

(*Looks at* **HENRY.**)

HENRY. What? Oh, yes. We've been discussing – the –

MARJORIE. The soap operas.

HENRY. The one about the old doctor that got the cheerleader pregnant then tried to give her an abortion in the back seat of his Buick?

ABE. Buick? Show me a doctor drives a Buick. It was a Mercedes.

HENRY. Okay, a Mercedes. Anyway, the girl decides to go see her priest. Or maybe you're going to tell me she went to see her rabbi, Abe.

ABE. It was a priest. Jewish girls don't get into such trouble.

HENRY. So anyway, the girl –

MARY. Thank you, Henry. Maybe if I ever get a little free time I'll watch it with you.

(*She turns to go.*)

MARJORIE. Goodnight, Mary. Have a good time tonight.

MARY. (*She turns to leave. Turns back.*) By the way, Marjorie. We moved Mrs. Murphy up to the second floor this evening. You won't have a roommate for a while. As soon as we find someone suitable, we'll let you know.

(*She exits.*)

MARJORIE. So, Mrs. Murphy has been promoted to the second floor. I don't know why they just don't bury the poor thing.

HENRY. What do you mean? They make a lot more money off the government from the folks on the second floor. They'll keep her up there for years.

MARJORIE. (*Opening her cosmetic bag.*) Okay, everybody. It's collection time.

DOTTIE. (*Putting the pills on the table.*) Here you go. Two yellows, a green, and a pink and white stripe.

ABE. I'll see your two yellows and raise you one white.

ROSE. Here's mine.

ABE. Three greens and two pinks. A full house. Rose is going to be tough to beat.

ISABEL. (*She stands.*) Damnit, you know how I hate to miss out on a good game. Here, Marjorie, take these –

MARJORIE. No, Isabel, you keep taking them until we find out what to do.

ISABEL. You know what's so ironic? I was a schoolteacher most of my life. I was preaching against drugs long before preaching against drugs was fashionable. If my students could see me now.

HENRY. And to think I just sat back and let them do this to you.

ISABEL. It wasn't your fault, Henry.

HENRY. I should have done something.

ISABEL. What?

HENRY. I don't know, something. I'm going to make this up to you, Izzy. I promise you. I'm going to get us a lawyer, tell him what they've done to you and Abe. And Rose here. This capsule they've been giving Rose,

(He takes a pill from the table.)

this is Thorazine, I found out more about it. It's not like valium or librium, it's one of the most potent tranquilizers made. It's intended for chronic psychotics!

ABE. No wonder you had a bladder problem.

ROSE. I don't know, but all of a sudden I feel alive again. First time in years. Maybe I'll die in the next minute. But at least I'll know I'm dead.

ABE. Look at this pile. I've got an idea. We'll sort out all the uppers and downers, take them out on the street and sell them. We can make a fortune. The geriatric connection.

ISABEL. Here. If Rose can stop so can I.

HENRY. Isabel.

ISABEL. No, listen to me. I never had a reason to quit before. I don't know how to say this, but you're the first family I've ever had. I'm so looking forward to – We've been talking about getting out of here for a week. If we're really going to do it, I'd like to do it soon.

MARJORIE. I don't know. Henry, what do you think?

HENRY. Next Saturday?

ABE. Saturday's the Sabbath. We can't move on Saturday. Let's do it Sunday.

DOTTIE. Sunday's the Lord's day.

MARJORIE. Does anyone have any religious objections to Monday?

ISABEL. That's another whole week.

HENRY. Tomorrow morning the entire staff has their weekly conference. Ten o'clock sharp.

MARJORIE. What do you all think, can we be packed up and ready by tomorrow?

DOTTIE. I'm already packed. I've been packed for years.

ABE. Take me five minutes.

HENRY. Okay, here's what we do. We sneak our bags down here in the morning then phone for a couple of cabs.

ABE. No cabs. I'm treating everybody to a limousine. A big black limousine. That's how I figured I'd leave this place and that's how we're going to do it. Joellen doesn't know this, but I still have my American Express Gold Card!

MARJORIE. There's no problem, is there Rose? I mean we can get into the house tomorrow.

ROSE. Tomorrow? Of course. The key is under the blue ceramic flower pot by the back porch.

ISABEL. Thank you. I love you. All of you. I do.

HENRY. Come get me if you need help.

ISABEL. I'll be all right.

(She exits.)

ABE. See you in the morning, everyone. I'm going to my room and create another masterpiece!

(He exits.)

DOTTIE. Come on, Rose. I'll give you a push.

*(Pushing **ROSE** toward the door.)*

DOTTIE. Wait until I show you my crystal. I have this set of cordial glasses, and when we get settled I'm going to buy some expensive French liqueur and you and I are going to get looped.

ROSE. *(Giggling.)* Oh, my.

*(**HENRY** and **MARJORIE** sit for a moment.)*

HENRY. Listen.

MARJORIE. What? I don't hear anything.

HENRY. That's just it. It hasn't been this quiet here since the day you arrived.

*(**MARJORIE** laughs and pokes **HENRY** in the ribs.)*

Tired?

MARJORIE. You kidding?

HENRY. Me either.

MARJORIE. Let's go outside.

HENRY. Probably cold out there.

MARJORIE. I won't mind. It's so nice to feel again, even cold will feel good.

HENRY. Here, I –

(He starts to help her with her chair.)

MARJORIE. I can do it. Turn out the lights. We'll be able to see the sky better.

(*He does. The room and terrace are bathed in moonlight. They go out onto the terrace.*)

Look at that moon.

HENRY. Cold?

MARJORIE. A little.

(**HENRY** *puts his arm around her.*)

That's nice.

HENRY. All those stars. Makes you feel insignificant, doesn't it.

MARJORIE. A little. But I feel less insignificant now than I did a few weeks ago.

HENRY. When I was a kid you know what I wanted to be? An inventor. It was all the rage back then. Perpetual motion machines, anti-gravity devices. When we get settled I'd like to try my hand at it again.

(**MARJORIE** *snuggles a little closer.*)

So, your roommate has been moved to the second floor.

MARJORIE. Yes. Poor Mrs. Murphy.

HENRY. Means you're going to be all alone in your room tonight.

MARJORIE. That's true.

HENRY. Not good for you to be alone.

MARJORIE. I'll be all right. Besides, I've got to pack.

HENRY. Need help?

MARJORIE. I can manage.

HENRY. Right.

(They're quiet for a moment.)

MARJORIE. *(Sitting up.)* Oh, my goodness!

*(Turning to **HENRY**.)*

You're making a pass.

HENRY. I hope I didn't –

MARJORIE. You poor man. I'm so sorry. You're right. Absolutely right. It would be terrible for me to spend the night alone.

HENRY. *(Smiles weakly.)* You don't think – think that this is just – lust?

MARJORIE. At our age, darling, lust is a virtue.

HENRY. Then come on, I'll – walk you home.

*(**HENRY** takes hold of **MARJORIE**'s chair and pushes her off.)*

Scene Two

(The recreation room the next morning. **MARJORIE, ROSE** *and* **DOTTIE** *are fidgeting anxiously.* **HENRY** *is standing in the hallway door.)*

DOTTIE. What time is it, Henry?

HENRY. Two minutes later than the last time you asked.

MARJORIE. Relax, Dottie. It's going to be all right.

DOTTIE. I said thirteen rosaries last night.

HENRY. Thirteen's an unlucky number. Say another one.

(Looking down the hall.)

Here comes Abe.

*(***HENRY** *waves.* **ABE** *hurries into the room. He carries a suitcase and two shopping bags.)*

ABE. I think we're home free. Most of the staff's already in the conference room.

HENRY. Stick those in here.

(Opening the door to the game closet. It's full of luggage, boxes, bags.)

ABE. I phoned the limo service first thing. They'll be here at ten o'clock sharp. I told them to park on the side street so we can see them from the terrace. Look at this.

(Taking a magnum of champagne from a shopping bag.)

Costs a hundred and fifty bucks a bottle. I've been saving it for a special occasion. To tell you the truth, I was beginning to think it was going to go to waste. Minute we get into that limo – pop!

(**ABE** *stuffs his bags into the closet.*)

DOTTIE. This is so exciting.

HENRY. Oh, and I called Con Edison. The power's on at your house Rose so we don't have to worry about that.

ROSE. Oh, that's –

ABE. (*Sitting.*) Whew. We all here?

HENRY. Everyone but Isabel. Thought I'd give her a couple more minutes.

> (**HENRY** *sits next to* **MARJORIE.** *Stares at her. She looks at him, smiles. He smiles back.* **ABE** *is watching them.*)

ABE. I stopped by your room last night, Henry. See if I could borrow a bag. You weren't there.

> (**HENRY** *doesn't comment.*)

I looked all over for you. I went back to your room three times.

HENRY. So?

ABE. So it's none of my business, right? I went by Marjorie's room. Heard a lot of heavy breathing in there.

MARJORIE. Oh, I was doing my exercises. Look, I can lift my – leg.

ABE. With that much breathing you should stand on your head.

DOTTIE. Mr. Waxman, not while I'm praying.

> (**ABE** *rushes up to* **DOTTIE**, *grabs her face and gives her a big kiss.*)

Oh! Mr. Waxman!

> (*She puts her rosary into her purse.*)

We are going to have fun, aren't we?

*(**ISABEL** enters carrying her bags. She is dressed in a fashionable suit, her hair is done, and makeup. **ABE** goes out on the terrace.)*

HENRY. Here she is.

ISABEL. Oh god, I made it.

MARJORIE. How are you feeling?

ISABEL. Look at me, I'm shaking like a leaf. But I got through the night. That's all that matters, I got through the night.

MARJORIE. You look beautiful.

ISABEL. Beautiful? When I tried to put on my eye makeup I outlined my ears.

MARJORIE. I hope we're not rushing this. Maybe a couple more days –

ISABEL. No! One more night staring at those four walls I'll go crazy. I'm all right. Really. Look.

(She takes a piece of Kleenex from her pocket and unwraps it.)

My morning pills. Add them to your collection, Marjorie.

*(**MARJORIE** takes the pills, opens her cosmetic bag and drops them in.)*

MARJORIE. Good thing we're leaving. My cosmetic bag's almost full.

ABE. *(Hurrying in.)* The limo! It's here! Look at that sucker, it's half a block long!

HENRY. *(Checking his watch.)* Ten o'clock on the nose. I'll make sure the coast is clear.

*(**HENRY** goes out the door into the hall. With the exception of **ROSE** everyone else goes to the game closet where they haul out suitcases,*

bags, boxes. Lots of ad-libbing, "That's mine,"
"Here I'll take that, you take the blue one," etc.
They turn, loaded down.)

MARJORIE. Ready, Rose?

(**ROSE** *nods.*)

DOTTIE. Then let's go for it.

(*They head toward the double doors.*)

ABE. I feel like Moses on his way to the Promised Land.

DOTTIE. Isn't this exciting?

(*As they reach the double doors, they swing
open.* **HENRY** *enters.*)

ABE. Come on, Henry, help me with this –

(**MARY** *follows* **HENRY** *into the room.*)

I just remembered. Moses never made it to the
Promised Land.

MARY. I should have a picture of this. No one would
believe me.

HENRY. I told you we're just –

MARY. Henry? Please. When I first learned of this, I thought
it was the most ridiculous thing I'd ever heard. You have
to admit, the thought of a bunch of senile, semi-invalids
wandering off by themselves is pretty preposterous.

DOTTIE. Call us all the names you like. It's not going to
stop us.

MARY. May I ask where you're going?

DOTTIE. We have a house.

MARY. A house?

MARJORIE. North Tyler. Check it out for yourself.

MARY. Oh, you mean Rose's house. Yes, she told me about it this morning.

*(General reaction. **ROSE** slumps into her chair.)*

Bright, sunny rooms, fireplace, maple trees in the front yard.

ISABEL. Rose? She told you?

MARY. Don't blame Rose. I've known you've been up to something all week. You've been about as subtle as kids with a cookie jar.

HENRY. Hang on, Marjorie. If we have to we'll run over her.

MARY. Do you know how foolish you are? How utterly foolish? You should be glad I found out. There isn't any house. Rose made it all up.

ABE. You're lying.

DOTTIE. Of course she is.

MARJORIE. She and her husband raised six children in it. We saw pictures.

MARY. Twenty-year-old pictures. The house was sold long before Rose even came here.

ABE. You're trying to trick us.

ISABEL. There has to be a house!

MARY. Isabel, please listen –

ISABEL. THERE HAS TO BE A HOUSE!

MARY. NO! NOW YOU LISTEN TO ME! Rose came here five years ago. When the state mental hospitals were dumping their elderly patients into nursing homes. She's been in and out of institutions ever since her husband died. The medication we've been giving her, Thorazine, is prescribed specifically for mental patients. Without it she lives in a world of fantasies. I'm telling you. If there is a house it only exists in Rose's mind.

MARJORIE. Rose?

> (**ROSE** *shrinks into herself.*)

ROSE. Oh, my.

ISABEL. You mean it's true? I'm going to kill her. I mean it, I –

HENRY. *(Holding her back.)* Take it easy, Isabel.

MARJORIE. Why, Rose?

ROSE. When you talked about finding another place, I...I was afraid you'd go off and leave me.

ABE. Dear God in heaven.

ROSE. It was a beautiful house. But when Papa died the rest of them, they began fighting over it. Wanted me to sell it. Give them the money. Papa built that house. When I said no, they told some judge I was crazy and had me sent away. I'm not crazy. Oh, I pretend sometimes. Like I pretend that they all live far away. But that's only so people won't ask why my children never visit. I'm sorry. I didn't mean to hurt anyone. I didn't.

> (**STEVEN** *enters.*)

STEVEN. *(To* **MARY**.*)* You mean it's true?

MARY. Ask them yourself.

STEVEN. *(To* **MARJORIE**.*)* The director of Sunset Terrace phoned me this morning. Told me you were instigating a – a –

HENRY. A jailbreak.

MARJORIE. Please, let's not have a scene.

STEVEN. Then it might be more pleasant if we went to your room.

MARJORIE. Another time, perhaps.

(She tries to move past **STEVEN.** *He takes hold of her chair and turns her back into the room.)*

STEVEN. I'm afraid I'll have to –

HENRY. Let go of her!

*(***HENRY** *grabs* **STEVEN***'s arm.* **STEVEN** *pushes* **HENRY** *who falls.* **MARJORIE** *turns and begins slapping at her son.* **STEVEN** *grabs her arms.)*

STEVEN. Stop it! I said, stop it!

*(***ABE** *starts toward* **STEVEN.***)*

MARY. Abe, you come over here and sit down. The rest of you. I want all of you to sit down!

DOTTIE. You can't give us orders any more!

MARY. I'm not ordering you, Dottie. I'm asking you as nicely as I can under the circumstances to please sit down.

DOTTIE. Well. As long as you're being civil, I will. I'll sit down. Come on, Abe.

MARJORIE. Henry, are you –

HENRY. *(Getting up.)* I'm all right, Marge.

STEVEN. The director also said you coerced these people into not taking their medications.

HENRY. No one coerced us.

MARY. You've put this home in an untenable situation. The legal implications alone, to say nothing of the well-being –

ISABEL. Yes, look at me.

ABE. My problem isn't a colon infection. It's those damn pills you've been giving me!

MARY. You see what I have to put up with, Mr. Kendrick? Their doctors prescribe medication and they blame me when it doesn't work.

ABE. Doesn't work? It works, it works!

STEVEN. Do you mind if we go outside?

(He takes her chair and pushes her out onto the terrace.)

MARY. *(At the door.)* I want the rest of you to wait right here until I get back.

(She exits as the focus shifts to the terrace.)

MARJORIE. I feel like some child whose parent has been called to school because she's misbehaved.

STEVEN. How do you think I feel? Were you really planning on running away? When I was here last Sunday, why didn't you say something?

MARJORIE. You'd have interfered.

STEVEN. Damn right I would have interfered.

MARJORIE. Which is why I didn't tell you.

STEVEN. What pills are they talking about?

MARJORIE. You heard the nurse. They're for our well-being. So what's next? They throwing me out of here?

STEVEN. No. But this morning, after they phoned, Patsy and I, we talked.

I – I mean we decided that it would be best for you to come and stay with us. You can have Melody's room. She can move in with Melissa.

MARJORIE. And what does your family say about this?

STEVEN. I can't lie to you, Mom. It'll be an adjustment.

MARJORIE. Thanks anyway.

STEVEN. What other choice do I have?

MARJORIE. Your choice? My choice. That's what we're talking about.

STEVEN. I can't just leave you here.

MARJORIE. Why not, you've done it before? Go on home. I promise I won't cause you any more trouble.

STEVEN. No, I can't permit –

MARJORIE. Damnit, will you listen to what I'm saying! I'm not asking your permission. I'm perfectly capable of deciding things for myself!

STEVEN. Like running off in search of an imaginary house!

MARJORIE. I made a mistake. I'm sorry.

STEVEN. Then come home with me.

MARJORIE. How can you be so smart one minute and so stupid the next? Times like this your father positively shines in you!

STEVEN. But it's all arranged.

MARJORIE. Then unarrange it. I spent the better part of my life living in a house where I was despised. I won't do that again.

>   (**STEVEN** *doesn't know what to say.* **MARJORIE** *reaches out with her left hand, takes* **STEVEN***'s hand.*)

Thank you, anyway. I love you.

>   (*She pulls him down and gives him a kiss.*)

And kiss the children for me.

STEVEN. You're sure about this?

>   (*He goes into the rec room as* **MARY** *returns with her pill cart.* **STEVEN** *says something to* **MARY** *then exits.* **MARY** *crosses to the terrace doors.*)

MARY. Marjorie? Would you care to join us?

*(She picks up a cup of pills and a container of water and goes to **ISABEL**. **MARJORIE** wheels herself into the room.)*

MARY. Isabel?

*(She offers **ISABEL** a cup. **ISABEL** hesitates, looks at the others who are all looking at her. After a long, painful moment, **ISABEL** takes the cup, swallows the pills. **MARY** goes to **ABE**.)*

Before you arrived here, Marjorie, this home was a model. Peace and contentment, that's what you felt when you opened the front door. It's going to be that way again. I promise you. Perhaps your inability to adjust is more serious than I thought. Perhaps you might be better off on the second floor. I'll let you know after I've spoken to your doctor.

ABE. I won't take these pills.

MARY. Would you prefer an injection? Under restraints?

*(After a moment, **ABE** swallows the pills. As **MARY** hands **MARJORIE** a cup, **HENRY** walks over and slaps the cup out of **MARY**'s hand. He then walks over to the pill cart and tips it over. He stares at **MARY** defiantly.)*

MARY. I see. Well, Henry. Looks as if I'll be adding your name to the medication chart along with the others.

(She turns to leave.)

I'll be back.

MARJORIE. Henry, why in god's name –

ABE. *(To **HENRY**.)* That was stupid.

HENRY. I know.

ISABEL. *(Beginning to feel the effects of the pills.)* But such a chivalrous gesture. Mueller was right, Marjorie. It was peaceful here before you arrived. We had accepted things. Now we're going to spend the rest of our lives – I mean it, Marjorie, I wish to god you'd never have come here!

ABE. Isabel!

ISABEL. I'm right and you know it! We were all better off!

(**MARJORIE** *wheels herself toward the bathroom.*)

You used to be my friend, Henry.

(*She follows* **MARJORIE** *to the bathroom.*)

Till she came. Batted those big blue eyes at you. She seduced you last night, didn't she? Surprised that I know? I went to your room. I wanted you to – play cards, something, anything to keep my mind off – But I was too late! That sweet little whore had gotten there first!

(**MARJORIE** *disappears into the bathroom.*)

HENRY. You nasty, old –

ABE. Don't, Henry. She doesn't know what she's saying. Come on, Isabel, sit down.

ISABEL. Sweet little whore.

ABE. Shut up.

(**ISABEL** *sits.*)

ROSE. (*Barely audible.*) Henry.

(*Louder.*)

Henry.

HENRY. Leave me alone, Rose.

ROSE. The pills, Henry.

HENRY. What are you talking about?

ROSE. Marjorie. Her cosmetic bag. It's full of pills.

HENRY. So?

(*It takes him a moment.*)

You don't think – No, it's crazy. She wouldn't –

(*He rushes to the bathroom door.*)

MARGE!

ABE. Come on, Henry. She's not that stupid.

HENRY. (*He pushes on the door.*) The door. It's stuck, she's jammed it somehow.

ABE. (*Hurrying to the door.*) Jammed it? Are you sure?

HENRY. Help me, Abe. Push!

ABE. I'm pushing, I'm pushing. Come on, Marjorie. Open the door.

DOTTIE. (*Starting for the hallway door.*) We'd better get help!

HENRY. No! You heard Mueller. She meant it. She'll send Marge upstairs.

(*Pounding on the door.*)

DAMN YOU, MARGE, IF YOU DO ANYTHING TO HURT YOURSELF I SWEAR I'LL –

(**MARY** *hurries into the room.*)

MARY. What on earth is going on here?

(*Everyone turns toward her. Freezes.*)

Answer me!

HENRY. Nothing.

MARY. I heard screaming and pounding.

ABE. Oh that.

MARY. Where's Marjorie?

HENRY. Marjorie?

ABE. *(To **HENRY**.)* Marjorie.

HENRY. Oh, Marjorie. Well, she –

ABE. She and Henry were having a fight.

HENRY. That's right. I was – I was – telling her what I thought of her for the fine mess she's gotten us all into.

MARY. Is that right?

ABE. You should have heard him. Boy did he lay into her.

HENRY. I'm sorry about the pill cart, Mary. I don't know what came over me.

ABE. You can go back to your meeting. All over anyway.

MARY. Where is she?

HENRY & ABE. Who?

HENRY. Marge? Oh. Bathroom.

DOTTIE. She's having a good cry, Mary. Henry was pretty rough on her. I think you should just leave her alone. She'll get over it.

MARY. I see.

(She waits a moment.)

I'd better talk to her.

HENRY. That really isn't nec –

MARY. *(Pushing on the door.)* Marjorie? It's me, I'd like to –

(Pushes again on the door.)

MARY. There's something wrong with this door.

ABE. Oh, yeah. It sticks sometimes. We've been meaning to tell –

MARY. Henry, help me with this door.

HENRY. Why don't you just leave her alone?

MARY. We do not have locked doors at Sunset Terrace! Now help me!

HENRY. Get away from that door!

MARY. All right, what's going on here?

HENRY. I said to get away from that door!

MARY. *(Turning, pounding on the door.)* MARJORIE, YOU OPEN THIS DOOR YOU HEAR ME!

HENRY. *(Pushing **MARY** away from the door.)* I TOLD YOU TO GET AWAY AND I MEANT IT!

MARY. I HAVE HAD ENOUGH OF THIS! I'M CALLING SECURITY! I'LL GET TO THE BOTTOM OF THIS AND WHEN I DO –

> *(**ROSE** who has been sitting against the wall gets up and yanks a fire alarm. The room is filled with a piercing clangor.)*

What on earth!

> *(**ROSE** quickly turns, hiding the pulled alarm switch behind her back.)*

> *(**ABE**, who has seen what happened, hurries to the hall door and opens it.)*

DOTTIE. Is it a fire? Are we –

ISABEL. Jesus, Mary and Joseph, now what?

ABE. *(At the hall door.)* I think I smell smoke. It's coming from the second floor!

MARY. Keep calm. It's nothing, I'm sure it's nothing.

> *(She hurries to the door, turns back.)*

All of you. Outside! Right now! We've practiced this drill before! Henry, get Marjorie out of there!

ISABEL. So somebody finally set fire to this fuckin' place! Wish it had been me!

MARY. Abe, you help Isabel.

> *(Hysterical.)*

Outside! I told you to get outside!

> *(She hurries out the door.)*

AND KEEP CALM!

DOTTIE. Isabel, get up. We've got to get out of here!

ABE. Relax, Dottie. There's no fire.

DOTTIE. What?

ABE. Rose! She pulled the alarm.

ROSE. I didn't know what else –

HENRY. Come on, Abe. Help me.

> *(The two of them charge the bathroom door, burst it open.* **HENRY** *rushes inside,* **ABE** *turns back into the rec room.)*

ABE. I think I dislocated my shoulder.

> *(**HENRY** emerges, pushing **MARJORIE**.)*

MARJORIE. LET GO OF ME!

HENRY. *(Searching her.)* The pills! Where are the pills!

MARJORIE. GET YOUR HANDS OFF ME!

HENRY. *(Finding the cosmetic bag. He shakes it.)* It's empty.

> *(Shaking her.)*

HENRY. YOU SWALLOWED THEM! HOW COULD YOU DO THIS? I LOVE YOU, GODDAMNIT! HOW COULD YOU –

MARJORIE. I DIDN'T SWALLOW THEM! I flushed them down the toilet.

HENRY. *(Stares at her a moment.)* Oh, god.

> *(Throws his arms around her and squeezes. We hear the sound of fire engine sirens.)*

ABE. *(From out on the terrace.)* Hey everybody! Come here, look.

DOTTIE. *(She goes to the terrace.)* What is it? Fire trucks?

ABE. Fire trucks, ambulances, cops. It's like a circus.

DOTTIE. *(Leaning over the railing.)* Look at it down there. It's pandemonium. Come here, Rose, look.

> (**ROSE** *walks out to the terrace.*)

Look what you've done. They've come to rescue us!

ABE. They haven't come to rescue us. They've come to put out the fire. Wait a minute. There's something else. Look. The limousine! IT'S STILL THERE!

ISABEL. The limousine?

> *(She gets up, runs to the terrace.* **HENRY** *pushes* **MARJORIE** *outside.)*

ABE. This is better than anything we could have planned.

> *(Grabbing* **ROSE**.*)*

Rose, you're beautiful!

ISABEL. The limousine. It is still there!

HENRY. By god, it is!

ABE. Henry, are you thinking what I'm thinking?

HENRY. You mean if we were to go down there and casually stroll up to that limousine, who the hell would notice?

ABE. Bingo!

ISABEL. You serious, Abe? You think we can still get out of here?

ABE. *(Rushing into the rec room.)* We gotta get out of here! That limo down there is costing me two hundred bucks an hour! Come on, Henry, help me with the bags. And hurry up. I'm starting to feel those damn pills!

ISABEL. Marjorie? I'm sorry.

> **(MARJORIE** *smiles, extends her arms.* **ISABEL** *and* **MARJORIE** *embrace.)*

ABE. *(Returning loaded with bags.)* Come on, you two! You can kiss and make up in the car!

DOTTIE. Where we going to go?

ISABEL. Who cares!

ABE. Everybody ready. Now act nonchalant. Like this.

> **(ABE** *walks off whistling and acting very nonchalant.* **DOTTIE, ISABEL** *and* **ROSE** *take up the whistle and follow* **ABE***'s lead.* **HENRY** *appears carrying a suitcase.)*

ROSE. *(As they disappear.)* Oh, my!

HENRY. *(To* **MARJORIE***.)* Ready.

> *(No response from* **MARJORIE***.)*

What's wrong?

MARJORIE. We're not going to get away with this, are we?

HENRY. What do you want me to say?

MARJORIE. The truth.

HENRY. We'll be lucky if we make it to the Nassau County line.

MARJORIE. Then maybe Isabel was right. Maybe you'd all have been better off if I hadn't come along and filled your heads with this silly pipe dream.

HENRY. Marge. That car down there, that limousine of Abe's, that's no silly pipe dream, that's real. Now you can sit here like a lump if you want to, but me, Margie – me, I'm going for a ride.

MARJORIE. Is that right?

HENRY. That's right.

MARJORIE. You'd go off and leave me behind?

HENRY. Who said anything about leaving you behind? You women! You're not happy until you drive a man nuts! But this time, sister, I'm not waiting!

(He pulls **MARJORIE** *to her feet.)*

MARJORIE. What do you think you're doing!

HENRY. I'm going to carry you to that damn limousine!

MARJORIE. Is that right?

HENRY. That's right!

MARJORIE. You men! One little roll in the sack and suddenly you're Arnold Schwarzenegger! I thought you had a hernia!

HENRY. By god, I do!

MARJORIE. In that case, dear –

(She kisses him.)

Don't you think it would be better if we walked?

(Grabbing the suitcase, **HENRY** *supports* **MARJORIE** *as the two of them walk off – laughing, chattering.)*

End of Play

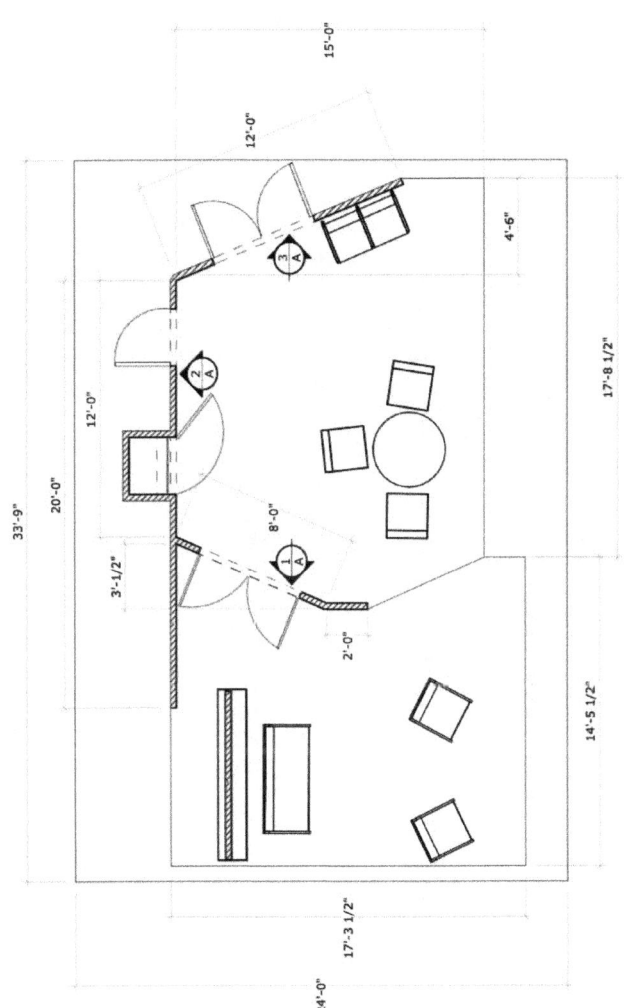